THE TERRIBLE TIGER

by JACK PRELUTSKY / Pictures by ARNOLD LOBEL

ALADDIN BOOKS

Macmillan Publishing Company / New York
Collier Macmillan Publishers / London

Aladdin Books
Macmillan Publishing Company
866 Third Avenue, New York, NY 10022
Collier Macmillan Canada, Inc.
First Collier Books edition 1973
First Aladdin Books edition 1989
Printed in the United States of America

10 9 8 7 6 5 4 3 2 1

Library of Congress Cataloging-in-Publication Data

Prelutsky, Jack
The terrible tiger/by Jack Prelutsky; pictures by Arnold Lobel
—1st Aladdin Books ed.   p.   cm.
Summary: A very hungry tiger eats the grocer, the baker, and
the farmer but makes a mistake when he eats the tailor.
ISBN 0-689-71300-2 [1. Tigers—Fiction. 2. Stories in rhyme.]
I. Lobel, Arnold, ill. II. Title.
PZ8.3.P9Te 1989
[E]—dc19   88-7901   CIP   AC

For Julie, with love

The terrible tiger woke at dawn,
he scratched his stomach,
he yawned a yawn.
He rubbed his eyes,
then yawned again,
and terribly left his terrible den.

He gnashed his teeth,
he swished his tail,
then set off hungrily down the trail,
and as he terribly loped along,
he terribly sang his terrible song.

"Oh, I'm the most terrible,
terrible, terrible
tiger that ever has been,
and anyone who comes my way
I'll surely swallow down today,
I'll eat him whether he's fat or lean,
for I am so terribly,
terribly mean.
Yes, I'm the most terrible,
terrible, terrible
tiger that ever has been."

The tiger hadn't traveled far,
not more than half a mile,
when he met the village grocer,
and he smiled a terrible smile.

"Good morning, good grocer,"
he terribly growled,
"it gladdens me greatly to greet you.
I've not had a bite
since eleven last night,
so, grocer, I'm going to eat you."

The trembling grocer fell down on his knees,
and begged in a terrified stutter,
"Oh, spare me, t-tiger, oh, tiger, oh, please,
I'll feed you ch-cheese and b-butter."

The tiger leered,
the tiger sneered,
he grinned a terrible grin.

"I'll eat your cheese, your butter, too,
and then, though you're all bones and skin,
before I've even wiped my chin
I'll pick you up and stuff you in
and eat you through and through."

And gobble, gobble, down he went,
for what the tiger said he meant.
He ate the grocer, butter and cheese,
and then, as quickly as you please
he turned and terribly loped along,
terribly singing his terrible song.

"Oh, I'm the most terrible,
terrible, terrible
tiger that ever has been,
and anyone who comes my way
I'll surely swallow down today,
I'll eat him whether he's fat or lean,
for I am so terribly,
terribly mean.
Yes, I'm the most terrible,
terrible, terrible
tiger that ever has been."

The tiger laughed a terrible laugh,
for there before his eyes
he saw the village baker
with his muffins, buns and pies.

"Good morning, fat baker,"
he terribly growled,
"it gladdens me greatly to greet you.
For I am a tiger, and terribly bad,
I just ate the grocer, and all that he had,
but I am still hungry, and so I must add
that, baker, I'm going to eat you."

"Oh, spare me, sir," the baker cried.
"I'll feed you bread and cake,
the finest biscuits, buns and rolls
that anyone can bake."

The tiger leered,
the tiger sneered,
he grinned from ear to ear.

"What is this foolishness I hear?
Oh, certainly I'll eat your bread,
but, baker, don't you be misled,
for then I'll also eat your head.
I trust that this is clear."

And gobble, gobble, down he went,
for what the tiger said he meant.
He ate the baker, round and fat,
and when he'd finished doing that
he turned and terribly loped along,
terribly singing his terrible song.

"Oh, I'm the most terrible,
terrible, terrible
tiger that ever has been,
and anyone who comes my way
I'll surely swallow down today,
I'll eat him whether he's fat or lean,
for I am so terribly,
terribly mean.
Yes, I'm the most terrible,
terrible, terrible
tiger that ever has been."

The tiger traveled on awhile
at a terrible, terrible pace,
till he spied a stocky farmer
and he glared into his face.

"Good morning, fine farmer,"
he terribly growled,
"it gladdens me greatly to greet you,
for all that I've eaten for breakfast today
are a grocer and baker I chanced to waylay,
so, farmer, say all that you feel you must say,
for, farmer, I'm going to eat you."

The farmer pleaded, "Set me free,
I'll feed you figs and berries,
the choicest pears and tangerines,
bananas, plums and cherries."

The tiger leered,
the tiger sneered,
he snorted through his nose.

"What is this nonsense you propose?
I'll eat your fruit, you poor buffoon,
but then before the clock strikes noon
I'll swallow you just like a prune,
your head and then your toes."

And gobble, gobble, down he went,
for what the tiger said he meant.
He called his terrible tiger call
and swallowed the farmer, figs and all,
then turned and terribly loped along
terribly singing his terrible song.

"Oh, I'm the most terrible,
terrible, terrible
tiger that ever has been,
and anyone who comes my way
I'll surely swallow down today,
I'll eat him whether he's fat or lean,
for I am so terribly,
terribly mean.
Yes, I'm the most terrible,
terrible, terrible
tiger that ever has been."

The tiger sped along the trail,
roaring his terrible roar.
He soon approached a tailor
and he thought, I've room for more.

"Good morning, old tailor,"
he terribly growled,
"it gladdens me greatly to greet you.
I gobbled the grocer, the baker to boot,
I finished the farmer along with his fruit,
so, tailor, don't bother to finish that suit,
for, tailor, I'm going to eat you."

The tailor took his glasses off
and put his needle down.
He looked up very thoughtfully
and frowned a gentle frown.

"Tiger orange, tiger black,
tiger thinks that I'm a snack
but, if tiger's not a dunce,
tiger will depart at once."

The tiger leered,
the tiger sneered,
he coughed and then began.

"You dare to threaten me, old man?
I'll breakfast on you anyhow,
I'll eat you as I would a cow,
in fact, I think I'll do it now
as quickly as I can."

And gobble, gobble, down he went,
for what the tiger said he meant.
He plucked the tailor off his stool
and ate him, thimble, thread and spool,
then turned and terribly loped along
terribly singing his terrible song.

"Oh, I'm the most terrible,
terrible, terrible
tiger that ever has been,

and anyone who comes my way
I'll surely swallow down today,
I'll eat him whether he's fat or lean,
for I am so terribly,
terribly mean.

Yes, I'm the most terrible,
terrible, terrible
tiger that ever has been."

But while the tiger loped along
in his terrible, terrible way,
the tailor lit a match and saw
the tiger's other prey.

The farmer sighed, the baker cried,
the grocer moaned, "Oh, me!"
The tailor put his glasses on.
"We'll see!" He smiled. "We'll see!

"It seems this tiger must be taught
to ask before he dines,"
and saying this he took his chalk
and drew some careful lines.

"Chalk and measure, scissors and pins,
thus the tailor's trade begins.
There's no need to be afraid,
now the tailor plies his trade.

"Scissors clap and scissors clip,
scissors, scissors, never slip.
Tailor's friends don't have to fear,
scissors let them out of here."

The tailor snipped, then snipped some more,
and soon to their delight,
the tailor freed the other three,
who bolted out of sight.

As soon as his friends had run safely away
the tailor climbed slowly outside
and spoke to the tiger, who sat in dismay
inspecting the hole in his hide.

"Tiger orange, tiger black,
tiger thought I was a snack
but, since tiger ate in haste,
tiger found his meal a waste.
Tiger does not have to brood.
I will mend him though he's rude,
for it makes a tailor moan
when a hole remains unsewn."

And so the tailor set to work
with fingers fleet and nimble
and stitched the terrible tiger up
with needle, thread and thimble.

The tiger sat silently
shaking his head
till the tailor had finished
and cut off the thread.

Then he sprang to his feet
with a terrible bound,
he roared at the tailor
and whirled around.

He gnashed his teeth,
he swished his tail,
and once again
sped down the trail,
and as he terribly loped along,
he terribly sang his terrible song.

"Oh, I'm the most terrible,
terrible, terrible
tiger that ever has been.
And anyone who comes my way
I'll surely swallow down today,
except that tailor,
for at best
he isn't easy
to digest.
But otherwise I'll eat them all,
I'll eat them whether they're short or tall,
I'll eat them whether they're fat or lean
for I am so terribly, terribly mean—

Yes, I'm the most terrible,
terrible, terrible
tiger that ever has been."